THE MYRTLE

BY

HILLARY DEPIANO

BASED ON THE FAIRY TALE FROM *THE TALE OF TALES* BY GIAMBATTISTA BASILE

ABOUT THE TALE OF TALES PROJECT

Giambattista Basile (1566–1632) wrote and compiled the 60 fairy tales within *The Pentamerone* (*Lo cunto de li cunti* in Neapolitan or *The Tale of Tales* in English) in Naples, Italy in the early 1600s. His sister, Adriana, published it in two volumes in 1634 and 1636 after his death. While not widely known, it's important historically because the Brothers Grimm later used it as the source for their far more famous fairy tale collection. *The Tale of Tales* contains the earliest known versions of fairy tales such as Sleeping Beauty, Cinderella, Rapunzel, Puss in Boots, Hansel and Gretel and more.

But I'm not interested in the stories everyone has heard of. I like the obscure ones, the weird ones lost to time. Why do we obsessively retell the same dozen fairy tales when there are plenty of other great ones we ignore?

It bothers me. So, since early 2013, I've been adapting these lesser-known tales for modern audiences to bring these stories back into circulation. I've modernized them with today's audiences in mind while still staying true to the spirit of the originals. Wherever possible, I also preserved the names from the original fairy tale and, where characters were unnamed, I've named them within the historical context and often with names from elsewhere in the Tales themselves.

This project is still ongoing. For the latest list of all the tales I've adapted from The Tale of Tales and what I'm working on next, visit HillaryDePiano.com.

BIBLIOGRAPHY

Basile, Giambattista (2007). Giambattista Basile's "The Tale of Tales, or Entertainment for Little Ones". Translated by Nancy L. Canepa, illustrated by Carmelo Lettere, foreword by Jack Zipes. Detroit, MI: Wayne State University Press. ISBN 978-0-8143-2866-8.

STANDALONE ONE-ACTS

There are standalone one-act versions of every fairy tale I've adapted from *The Tale of Tales*.

THE MYRTLE

30-40 minutes, 5 m 8 f (6-20+ performers possible)
A prince discovers his myrtle tree turns into a fairy maiden at sundown.

GOOSED!

(based on *The Goose*)
25-35 minutes, 2 m 6 f 8 any (11-20+ performers possible)
Two poor sisters rescue a golden goose but their sneaky neighbors want it for themselves.

ARM CANDY

(based on *Pintosmalto)*
35-45 minutes, 2 m, 4 f (5-7+ performers possible)
When a brilliant inventor builds the perfect husband out of sugar, he's stolen by a queen who wants him for herself.

THE FOURTH ORANGE

(based on *The Merchant* with characters from Carlo Gozzi's *The Love of Three Oranges*)
20-30 minutes, 4 m, 6 f, 5 any (7-20+ actors possible)
There were only supposed to be three oranges but Franceschina had to stick her nose where it didn't belong.

THE SHE BEAR

25-35 minutes, 2 m 2 f (4-10+ performers possible)
Is the prince losing his mind or has he really fallen in love with a bear?

VARDIELLO

10-15 minutes, 1 m, 1 f, 2 any
How much damage can one half-wit do before his mother gives him the boot?

Want to combine plays to make an evening's entertainment?
You'll find shortened versions of the most popular fairy tales in this fun and fantastical full length!

THE FOURTH ORANGE
AND OTHER FAIRY TALES YOU'VE NEVER EVEN HEARD OF
100-120 minutes, 25w 12m 11any (11 to 60+ performers possible)
It's bedtime bedlam when a washed-up clown tries to sell three unruly princesses on something other than their fairy tale favorites.

Looking for something even more flexible?
Mix and match the tales above to create an evening's entertainment and I'll provide interstitial material and opening and closing scenes to connect the tales together no matter what combination you choose!

For more information about this custom option, email Hillary DePiano.

THE MYRTLE

The Myrtle premiered on November 16-18, 2017 at Rutgers Preparatory School in Somerset, NJ with the following cast and crew.

TRUFFALDINO...Nate Lyles
LA GIARDINIERA.......................................Carla Evans
MIDWIVES...Livia Lee
....Aarushi Roperia
....Emma Sperr
THE MYRTLE...Samantha Barbato
KING MARCHIONE...................................Qingshi Meng
LORENZO...Daniel Forte
VENDRAMINA...Kaylah Holmes
MEA..Christal Onyekwere
DEA...Daria Bresnick
PRINCE COLA..Sachin Mathew
CHAMBERMAID.......................................Selena Adrianzen
ROCCO...David Chen

ENSEMBLE

Esha Mehta, Kevin Tao, LongGe (Andrea) Wang, Paris Townsell, Richard Xiang, Skyllar Capuno, Tabetha Kiraz, Téa Guarino

Directed by..Cora M. Turlish
Assistant Directed by..............................Skyllar Capuno
Student Assistant Director......................Tara Viswanath
Set Design by...Erin Drakoulis
Set Construction Coordination by...........Derrick Laurion
Lighting Design & Direction by..............Michael Nardulli
Costumes by...Christina Kratzman
Stage Managed by....................................Sunny Chen
Assistant Stage Manager.........................Aela Williams
Lighting Board Operator..........................Jamie Chen
Sound Board Operator.............................Michael Slass
Backstage Crew..David Chen, Jonina Yang
Publicity Art...Skyllar Capuno
Make Up Coordinator..............................Kuntal Thakkar

Set Construction
David Chen, Jamie Chen, Jesse Cross, Liz Gambacorta, Zac Gambacorta, Libby Gilfeather, Nya Johnson, Val Lazarczyk, Matthew Romage, Rishie Seshadri, Michael Slass, Emma Sperr, Jonina Yang

Make-up
Aaditi Ahlawat, Amrin Ashraf, Mahima Chaluvadi, Rachel Emmett, Isabelle Fehl, Nithya Goel, Lauren Hanna, Catherine Harbour, Ava Margolis, Eloise Meek, Kuntal Thakkar, Tara Viswanath

~

The playwright extends her greatest heartfelt thanks to the following groups who workshopped early versions of this play. It is thanks to your excellent cast and crews that this show is what it is today!

SIERRA HIGH SCHOOL
JANUARY 11-20TH, 2017

RUTGERS PREPARATORY SCHOOL
NOVEMBER 16-18TH, 2017

ANNIE WRIGHT SCHOOLS
APRIL 26-27TH, 2018

PRODUCTION NOTES

Please don't hesitate to contact me [(hillary@hillarydepiano.com)](mailto:hillary@hillarydepiano.com) for any reason. I'm here to help!

IMPROVISATION

In the spirit of the slapstick of classic Italian theatre and commedia dell'arte tradition that inspired these adaptations, you're encouraged to put your own spin on all comedic bits and fights and to explore the physical comedy through improvisation. If you can come up with something funnier than the stage directions describe, go for it! I'm even happy to approve changes in dialog or more modern references, just run it by me first. For performer safety, avoid injury by always making sure you finalize all physical routines before the show opens. While you certainly don't have to, you're welcome to perform the show in masked commedia style if desired.

CONTENT

While this fairy tale is PG as written (as most classic fairy tales are), I'm happy to work with schools and other groups who may need to tone it down to be able to perform it. Be it language or situational, please email me (hillary@hillarydepiano.com) with any issues you run into. I'll do my best to help you find a workaround.

CASTING NOTES

I encourage blind casting in all cases where it comes to race, gender, body type, etc. If you're in a casting pickle, please email me to explain your casting needs and I'll help you out. I can give you alternate character names and lines or grant permission to change character genders as needed, whatever we need to do to make it happen.

CAST SIZE

While I've only specified two sisters for VENDRAMINA, the original tale has seven sisters total. If you'd like to get more performers involved, you may cast additional sisters named LEA, BEA, KEA, and ZEA and divide MEA and DEA's lines up amongst these roles. You're also welcome to increase the number of midwives, chambermaids, lords and ladies of the court, and gardeners as needed. For a smaller cast, performers can each play multiple roles.

Photos courtesy of Sierra High School Drama, January 2017

Photos by Scot Whitman, Rutgers Prep, November 2017

CHARACTERS
(In order of appearance)

TRUFFALDINO, clown who acts as narrator for the tale
LA GIARDINIERA, peasant woman and talented gardener
BOOMING VOICE FROM THE HEAVENS
MIDWIVES
THE MYRTLE, fairy by night, myrtle tree by day
KING MARCHIONE , father of Prince Cola
LORENZO, adviser to the royal family
VENDRAMINA, social climber
MEA, Sister to Vendramina
DEA, Sister to Vendramina
PRINCE COLA, socially awkward prince
CHAMBERMAID
ROCCO, head royal gardener
GARDENERS

SETTING
A fairytale kingdom.

TIME
The imaginary past.

THE MYRTLE

SCENE 1

(The clown Truffaldino enters with a dusty old book, the cover of which reads, "The Tale of Tales or Entertainment for Little Ones by Giambattista Basile." He sits as if to read the audience a bedtime story.)

TRUFFALDINO

OK, kids, let's go. Teeth all brushed? Bathroom business all attended to? Good! Then let's get this bedtime story underway! Look what I found up in the attic for us to read tonight.

(He reads the title off the front)

"The Tale of Tales or Entertainment for Little Ones by Giambattista Basile." It's an old book of fairy tales. Yeah, it's got all the popular princesses and well worn standards and whatnot, but we're not reading any of those tonight. Why? Because you've already heard them a billion times and I'm sick of them. It's time to give the rest of them a chance to shine.

(He opens to a story)

Like... this one. It's called, "The Myrtle." And it's got everything you could want in a fairy tale: drama, comedy, romance, and a surprising amount of gratuitous violence. So let's get started.

(As he beings to read, La Giardiniera's cottage appears)

Once upon a time, there lived a woman with a gift for greenery called La Giardiniera. Her garden was the envy of all the land and the flowers she sold at market had no equal in all of Miano. But while her plants flourished, she wanted a nursery of a different kind. For though she had never cared for a husband, she had always longed for a child.

LA GIARDINIERA

Oh, heavens!

TRUFFALDINO

She'd call each evening...

LA GIARDINIERA

Please send me a child of my own...

TRUFFALDINO

Night after night...

LA GIARDINIERA

If I could just have a little baby...

TRUFFALDINO

...she would plead with the sky...

LA GIARDINIERA

I wouldn't care, even if it were only a sprig of a myrtle.

TRUFFALDINO

Until one day...

LA GIARDINIERA

Come now, I beg of you--

BOOMING VOICE FROM THE HEAVENS

Fine. Fine! Your wish is granted! Just stop bugging us!

(She reveals her large pregnant belly as she moves to the bed, straining with labor pains. Midwives flutter around her, getting ready for the birth.)

TRUFFALDINO

She grew large with child and, when it came her time, the midwives watched astonished as she gave birth to a--

MIDWIFE

Congratulations! It's a... bush?

(They wrap the tree like a baby and give it to the old woman who cradles it lovingly.)

ANOTHER MIDWIFE

A myrtle tree! That's a new one.

MIDWIFE

Oof. That had to hurt on the way out.

LA GIARDINIERA

She's absolutely perfect!

ANOTHER MIDWIFE

Mmmhmm. Of course it is, lady.

> *(They snicker as they exit. La Giardiniera takes the sprig and transfers it to a large ornamental pot.)*

LA GIARDINIERA

Pay them no mind, little one. I love you just as you are. There. Nice and comfy.

TRUFFALDINO

She kept the sprig in an ornamental pot and tended it with as much care and attention as if it were a human child. The tree flourished and tiny buds burst into beautiful flowers.

> *(La Giardiniera kisses the tree goodnight and settles into her bed. She puts out the lamp, a shaft of moonlight across her bed the only light.)*

Each day she brought the tree outside to feast on the rays of the sun and, each night, she brought it to her bedside where she sang it soft songs until she fell asleep. Then, one night, something wondrous happened.

LA GIARDINIERA

> *(waking)*

What's that? Who's there?

> *(She gasps.)*

Little one? Can it be?

MYRTLE
(unseen, a child's voice)

Mama?

(The cottage scene disappears.)

SCENE 2

TRUFFALDINO

The years passed happily until one day, the King and his court happened by on their way to hunt.

> *(Daytime at the cottage, many years later. The myrtle has bloomed into a beautiful flowered tree which sits outside the cottage in the sun. The court trots by and King Marchione pauses in front of the myrtle.)*

KING

Lorenzo! I find myself taking a fancy to this beautiful plant. It would be the perfect gift to welcome the prince home from his travels. Have one of the hangers-on grab it for me.

LORENZO

You mean purchase it, sire?

KING

I didn't but if you're going to keep doing that thing with your face... Here.

> *(Hands him a bag of gold.)*

No price is too high! I'd give one of my eyes for it. Well, one of their eyes, anyway.

LORENZO

As you wish.

> *(The King gallops off. Lorenzo pulls Mea, Dea, and Vendramina aside before they can follow with the rest of the train. They are dressed to seduce in an overdone approximation of courtly dress.)*

LORENZO

Vendramina, you've made it clear you and your sisters seek the attentions of the royal family. Here's your chance to win it. The King desires that myrtle as a gift for the Prince's return. Take this gold and secure it for him.

MEA

But we'll miss the whole hunt!

(Vendramina kicks her.)

VENDRAMINA

What my silly sister means to say is it would be an honor and our dearest pleasure to serve his royal highness in this or any other way he might desire.

(She lays it on really thick)

LORENZO

Yes. Well. I will, uh... Just see that it's done.

(Lorenzo exits.)

DEA

What's your scheme, Vendramina?

VENDRAMINA

Don't you fools listen? That myrtle is to be a gift for Prince Cola himself! Such beauty delivered from our hands? The prince cannot help but notice us. There's bound to be one of us he fancies enough to marry and then the new princess can bring the rest up with her.

MEA

Well, then what are we waiting for? Let's swipe that myrtle!

DEA

But the King gave us gold.

VENDRAMINA

Which we'll keep as our tip. Come, quickly now, while no one is around.

(They grab the potted myrtle. As they disappear with it offstage, La Giardiniera appears in the doorway, disheveled from sleep.)

LA GIARDINIERA

Who's out here jabbering on while I'm trying to--

(She realizes the tree's gone.)
No! Gone? I won't rest until I find you! I'll run my feet bloody if that's what it takes! Myrtle!

(She runs offstage)

SCENE 3

TRUFFALDINO

La Giardiniera pursued as fast as her old legs would allow but the sisters were faster and stole the myrtle back to the palace. That night, Prince Cola returned from his travels and the King presented his son with the purloined plant. Prince Cola was so enamored with it that he carried the pot with the greatest care in the world into his own chambers and placed it in the balcony.

(The prince's chambers at early evening. Prince Cola Marchione enters carrying the myrtle, with Lorenzo close behind.)

LORENZO

Are you certain I can't help you, Prince Cola? You've traveled so far today.

PRINCE COLA

I've got it.

(He places it on the balcony in his room.)
Perfect. Sun and moonlight both touch that terrace so I'll be able to gaze upon it's magnificence whenever I desire. Look at it! Have you ever seen such a miracle, a jewel, the teardrop of an angel reflecting a beautiful dove...

LORENZO

It is lovely.

PRINCE COLA

Lovely? It's like looking at love itself. A miracle of nature, like dawn cresting a hill at sunrise, the moon full and glassy on a still lake, the eye of a falcon as it--

LORENZO

Your majesty.

PRINCE

I was doing it again, wasn't I?

LORENZO

You were going on a bit, yes.

PRINCE COLA

It's been a while since I had anyone to talk to.

LORENZO

I thought you handpicked your companions for this trip.

PRINCE COLA

I did and good fellows all, it's just that--

KING
(bellowing from offstage)
Where is that blasted robe?

LORENZO

Forgive me. I must attend to your father. You know what he's like.

PRINCE COLA

Yeah, a royal pain.

LORENZO

It is good to have you back home.

(A woman shrieks offstage. The King bellows from offstage again.)

KING

Aha! Giving yourself an eyeful of the royal jewels, are you?

LORENZO

I must go. Goodnight, Prince Cola.

> *(He bows and leaves. The prince takes off his crown and jacket.)*

PRINCE COLA

A bow even from Lorenzo and he's known me since I was a baby! I ought to just prop this outfit up and wheel it out there on a dummy whenever they feel like showing me off. There's not one of them that would notice. All anyone cares about is the crown, they don't give a fig for who's underneath.

> *(He can't stand to look at it. He tosses his jacket over the crown and heads to bed.)*

SCENE 4

> *(Prince Cola plops down on his bed and puts out the lamp. Dusk gives way to evening. The room is dark apart from a small bit of moonlight from the terrace. A figure starts sneaking across the room, dragging something. The prince wakes and jumps from his bed.)*

Ah ha! What's this? Some chamber-boy come to lighten my purse? Some imp looking to pull my bedclothes off? Have at you!

> *(Blinded in the dark, he lunges at nothing and falls flat on his face.)*

Slippery scoundrel!

> *(He dives again, this time coming close enough that the intruder yelps. He zeroes in on this, tackling her to the ground. They struggle.)*

There! Now, to get a look at you.

> *(He lights the lamp revealing a young woman, her*

hair tied to his arm.)

PRINCE COLA

Who...?

MYRTLE

What kind of a fiend binds someone with their own hair?

PRINCE COLA

I... Is that not a thing? Wait, let me get that for you.

(He unties her hair. The moment the Myrtle is free, she puts as much distance between them as possible.)

MYRTLE

Get away from me, villain!

PRINCE COLA

Villain? You're the one sneaking around my chamber in the middle of the night. I should call for the guards.

MYRTLE

Guards? Where are we? Where have you taken me?

(She tries to drag the pot to the door.)
I must go.

PRINCE COLA

Ah ha! You are a thief after all! That mine!

(He goes for it.)
It's empty! What did you do with my myrtle?

MYRTLE

How dare you! I assure you, human, I belong to no one but myself.

PRINCE COLA

Human?

(He takes a better look at her)

Oh my... You're a fairy!

MYRTLE

I am. Do not pretend you are surprised. You knew what I was. Why else would you have kidnapped me?

PRINCE COLA

What are you talking about?

MYRTLE

The myrtle. You deny you stole it?

PRINCE COLA

It was a gift from my father.

MYRTLE

Then he stole it.

PRINCE COLA

Treason! My father would never... would probably not have... Actually, that does sound like something my father would do.

MYRTLE

I do not have time for this. The moon is rising, and I must find my way home before dawn. Give me back my pot.

PRINCE COLA

But where is the myrtle?

MYRTLE

I am the myrtle, you fool.

PRINCE COLA

You're the myrtle?

MYRTLE

I was only a child. I had never granted a wish before. But she was all alone and so was I so, when they sent me, I thought... But I botched the spell. The plant and I, we are bound. It's too strong in the sun and it pushes me under. But moonlight is a time of magic and, while the tree sleeps, I live. It's only half a life but we made the best of it, her and I.

You see?

PRINCE COLA

You're the myrtle?

MYRTLE

Are you even listening? Plant or person, fairy or foundling, my mother loved me for what I am and now she's all alone again. I have to get back to her before the sun rises and I'm rooted once more. You must release me!

PRINCE COLA

You are not my prisoner.

MYRTLE

Then tell me the way back to the cottage in the woods and I shall be on my way.

PRINCE COLA

You're going to have to be more specific than that. This whole land is woods with cottages in them. Take a look.

(She looks out the balcony)

MYRTLE

Oh, no! Our forest. It could be anywhere! What can I do? I will never find my way back home now!

PRINCE COLA

Please, don't cry. My father is like an elephant sometimes, trampling lives under his massive foot without realizing what he's doing. Whatever confusion has led us to this moment, know that I am hereafter your ally in setting things right.

MYRTLE

Your offer is kind, but even if you were the prince with all the power in the realm, my mother is just one forgotten person in a land of thousands.

PRINCE COLA

What do you mean? I am the... You don't know who I am.

MYRTLE

I do not. How can I know if you can even be trusted?

PRINCE COLA

Because I swear to you on the blood that pulses through my veins that I will do you no harm. You have my word on the sea that pools behind my eyelids when I think of your plight, on the fluttered wings of spring that dance in my stomach when I look at your eyes, on the heart that hammers against my chest like a lone apple trapped in a barrel as it rolls down a dew covered hill at the, uh...

(She's staring at him.)

Yeah.

MYRTLE

Your manner is strange. But there is something appealing in it. And I find that I do trust you.

PRINCE COLA

Then let me help you! I will send for maps, scouts, whatever it takes to help you find your way home.

MYRTLE

Very well. Perhaps fortune will smile on us and I will not be away from my mother for more than a single day.

SCENE 5

(The Prince and Myrtle pour over maps on a table in the prince's chambers.)

TRUFFALDINO

They began their search at once, but so much of the land was covered in the same dense forest of the kind she remembered that the task seemed impossible. As morning dawned, they were no closer than they were at the start. It was the same the next morning and the next until the myrtle despaired of ever finding her mother while Prince Cola despaired of the day that they would.

(The Prince and Myrtle accidentally touch. They

have a moment. It nearly becomes a kiss, but the myrtle's hand slips on the maps on the table, spilling them on the floor. They scramble to pick them up.)

PRINCE COLA

Whoops, let me--

MYRTLE

It's fine, I-- Oh!

(She stares at one of the maps.)

PRINCE COLA

What is it?

MYRTLE

It's... it's nothing. The sun is nearly up. I should get back to my pot before it rises. Forgive me, I must go.

(She exits to the balcony. Prince Cola watches her go.)

PRINCE COLA

Must you?

SCENE 6

(The next day. The Prince has passed out on the bed fully dressed.)

TRUFFALDINO

Prince Cola was exhausted, fulfilling his duties to the kingdom by day and working through the night to keep his promise to the Myrtle. When he did sleep, he slept fitfully, knowing the day their search succeeded was the day that he would lose the woman he loved.

(The King comes in like Boom! Prince Cola wakes so violently he falls out of bed.)

KING

Ha! They said I'd find your lazy butt still abed!

PRINCE COLA

Aah! Father?

KING

I grow tired of your sloth, boy! Since you've been back you lay about most the day, walking like the dead the rest. You've barely been in the court.

PRINCE COLA

I came to that council meeting.

KING

You fell asleep!

PRINCE COLA

Well, it was a boring meeting.

KING

A man was stabbed during that meeting!

PRINCE COLA

I-

KING

In his bare ass!

PRINCE COLA

Really? How--

KING

You are the heir to the throne and I will not tolerate you shirking your duties. There's a long day of meetings and greetings ahead and I'm not doing them alone again. You're coming with me.

PRINCE COLA

But-- Ow! Ow!

(The King drags him out of the room by his ear.)

SCENE 7

(The court. Lords and ladies mill about including Mea, Dea and Vendramina. The King unceremoniously shoves the prince into his throne. Lorenzo brings Prince Cola some coffee but he falls asleep anyway. Mea, Dea and Vendramina approach.)

VENDRAMINA

Your majesty, how we've missed your handsome face.

(Prince wakes. They have him surrounded.)

PRINCE COLA

I'm awake! I mean, um... Hello?

DEA

You're so tired, your highness. Has something been keeping you up all night?

MEA

I wish it was me.

(They're all getting handsy. The Prince tries unsuccessfully to escape.)

PRINCE COLA

Ladies, please. You're going to rip me apart.

VENDRAMINA

Wouldn't that be wonderful? If only we could tear you into little bits so we could each have our own princely piece.

PRINCE COLA

Uh...

DEA

Did you like the myrtle we got you?

PRINCE COLA

The myrtle? Father couldn't remember... It was you?

MEA

Yes! And doesn't the loveliness of its blossoms make you want to do some pollinating of your own?

PRINCE COLA

Please. You must tell me where you got it. I will give you whatever you desire.

VENDRAMINA

Of course, anything for you, your highness. We bought it from a flower seller in Miano.

PRINCE COLA

Miano! Ladies, I am in your debt.

MEA

Ooo! And we cannot wait to collect.

(The prince starts for the exit.)

DEA

Was that wise? What if he realizes we stole it?

VENDRAMINA

Then we'll just have to distract him. Come. Let's go get some shovels. I have a most wonderful idea.

(They exit. The King catches the prince before he can leave.)

KING

Where do you think you're off to?

PRINCE

It's nearly nightfall, I must--

KING

That's it! There's only one thing you must do and that's whatever I order you to. There's a boar terrorizing the lowlands. And you're going to go and kill it.

PRINCE

Me? Couldn't you send some someone else?

KING

Of course I could! But it does the people good to see the crown running around shaking a spear at their problems. Makes the monarchy seem a little more real. Lorenzo, have them ready his horse.

LORENZO

As you wish, sire.

PRINCE

What, now? But I can't go now, I've got--

KING

You can and you will.

PRINCE

But--

KING

I will not be disobeyed! You're leaving within the hour and that's final!

(The King storms out.)

PRINCE COLA

The myrtle! There's hardly any time!

(He runs off.)

SCENE 8

(The prince's chamber. He races in.)

PRINCE COLA

I know where she is! Your mother! We did it! We've found her at last!

(He checks the balcony. The myrtle is still a tree. He

yells at the sun.)
Oh, hurry up and set already!

> *(He goes to the maps, pausing on the one the myrtle*
> *was staring at the night before.)*
...how can this be?

> *(The sun has set. The myrtle fairy enters from the*
> *balcony. He turns to her.)*
The village of Miano. You knew. For how long?

MYRTLE

Since last night. I knew it would mean goodbye and I couldn't... I have developed such an affection for you over these nights and I found I wasn't ready to part with you.

PRINCE COLA

You? For me? Oh, dearest fairy, can it be? For my love for you has burned like a fire made from a thousand suns, with a passion as hot as the bright red metal of a master-smith, and even so it is as strong as a thousand oxen each of them with legs of iron and a horns of polished--

> *(She kisses him.)*
What does that mean?

MYRTLE

It means shut up.

PRINCE COLA

Oh.

MYRTLE

But it also means yes. I will marry you. If I wait for you to get to the question, we'll both be gray.

> *(They embrace.)*

PRINCE COLA

Oh, my love! I never want to leave your arms!

> *(in the distance, the King bellows)*

KING

Cola!

PRINCE COLA

Although, I actually have to go right now.

MYRTLE

Go? Where?

PRINCE COLA

My father is sending me on a hunt. For a wild beast that's terrorizing the kingdom, appropriately enough, since that's what he is.

(The King bangs on the door.)

KING

I heard that! Open this door!

MYRTLE

Oh no! How long will you be gone?

PRINCE COLA

I cannot say. But our party is to travel through Miano. I can go to your mother myself and declare my intentions. My men will escort her back here in all the comforts of a queen so that you two may have your reunion.

MYRTLE

Then go. Complete your father's errand as quickly as you can and come right back to my arms.

PRINCE COLA

The only way I can bear the thought of being parted from you is because I know we'll be married at once upon my return. There is a chambermaid I trust. I'll tell her all. She'll see to it that you're watered and cared for.

(King bangs on the door again.)

KING

Boy! I'll break it down if I have to!

PRINCE

I must go. He's not joking about breaking it down. It's already been replaced twice.

MYRTLE

I'll stay hidden until my mother arrives. We need a sign. This silver bell.

(There's a small bell on the prince's bedside table.)
Tell my mother to ring it when she arrives so that I will know it is safe to reveal myself. Until then, my love, farewell.

(She disappears onto the balcony as the prince opens the door and the King nearly topples in.)

KING

Uff-- There you are!

PRINCE COLA

I was coming-- Ow! You know, I'm a grown-- OK! OK! OW!

(The King drags him out by his ear again.)

SCENE 9

(As soon as the prince is gone, Mea, Dea, and Vendramina burst through the floor covered in dirt, with shovels, pick axes and other digging implements in tow. They are whispering, thinking Prince Cola is asleep in his bed.)

VENDRAMINA

At last! We're in!

MEA

So this is Prince Cola's bedroom.

DEA

Isn't he going to be angry that we dug a tunnel from our house into his chambers without asking?

MEA

Nonsense! You saw how pleased he was with us in the ballroom today.
He practically asked us to.

VENDRAMINA

Besides, what hot blooded man wouldn't want his lovers to be able to
pop in for a secret tryst whenever he desired?

MEA

How about I slip into bed with him right now and play at a little Mute
Sparrow.

DEA

Wait. The bed's empty! He's not here.

VENDRAMINA

What? It can't be!

*(She tosses the covers off the bed, overturning the
bell on the bedside table. The myrtle fairy calls from
the balcony.)*

MYRTLE

Mother?

MEA

Who said that?

MYRTLE

...my love? Are you back so soon?

DEA

There's someone out on the balcony.

(She pulls back the curtain revealing the myrtle.)
What's this?

MYRTLE

Who--?

VENDRAMINA

Some trollop sneaking into the prince's bed chamber hoping to seduce him in the night!

MEA

Absolutely shameful.

DEA

Yeah! That is our shtick.

MYRTLE

The prince? Whatever are you talking about? These rooms belong to my fiancée.

DEA

Fiancé? We're too late!

MEA

All that primping!

DEA

All that scheming!

MEA

All that digging!

BOTH

And for nothing!

(They sob.)

VENDRAMINA

Stop it! Pull yourself together. She's lying. She has to be.

MYRTLE

How dare you!

VENDRAMINA

I've never seen you with him, not even once.

MYRTLE

We were only engaged tonight, there wasn't even time to introduce me to his father let alone make it public before--

DEA

So, no one but the prince knows about you?

MYRTLE

Well, yes, but--

MEA

I'll bet I can make even him forget that soon enough with a little game of Stone in Your Lap.

MYRTLE

Stay away from me. I don't like the looks on your faces.

VENDRAMINA

We've worked too long and hard for this prize to let you snatch it from us at the last minute, girl.

MYRTLE

Stop it. Don't come any closer.

MEA

No one will ever know you were engaged to the prince.

DEA

Not if you never make it out of this room alive.

VENDRAMINA

Tear her apart.

TRUFFALDINO

They advanced on the fairy, and she was soon overpowered. They pulled at her, each wanting to be the one to end her and, in their lust for blood, they tore her into pieces.

(They attack her. The more ridiculously gory it gets, the better. They can back her onto the balcony, so the violence plays out in shadows against the curtain. They freeze as someone tries the door.)

MEA

What's that?

DEA

There's someone at the door.

VENDRAMINA

Come, quickly! Before we're discovered!

(They exit through their hole, covering it behind them. A chambermaid enters and discovers the carnage. She freezes.)

TRUFFALDINO

The poor chambermaid came upon a gruesome scene: torn limbs, bits of skin, chunks of bone and tooth strewn about the room, blood pooling in the...

(He looks at the audience.)

What? ... Too much? But it says right here on the cover, "Entertainment for little ones." Anyway, the girl rolled up her sleeves and got to work collecting body parts, scraping skin off the floor and mopping up the blood. Once she had gathered it all into the myrtle's pot, she gave the whole mess a generous sprinkle of water. Then, with a nod, she promptly ran screaming from the palace never to be heard from again.

(The chambermaid collects all the body parts into the pot, waters it, closes the balcony curtain and exits as described.)

CHAMBERMAID

Aaaaaaaaaaaaaaaah!

SCENE 10

TRUFFALDINO

By morning, the gruesome pile had transformed back into the myrtle tree, but it was a broken, dead thing.

(The next morning. Lorenzo comes to check on the

myrtle. He discovers the dead tree.)

LORENZO

Ahh! The prince's beloved myrtle! Dead? Someone call for the gardeners! Oh, if the tree cannot be revived, they'll have my head.

(An army of gardeners file in with Rocco at the head. They puzzle and fuss over the myrtle tree as Lorenzo paces. Day turns to night and back again.)

TRUFFALDINO

He sent for the palace gardeners and they employed every trick they knew. As day turned to night again and again and the plant stayed the same lifeless stick, things looked bleak indeed.

LORENZO

This isn't working. Go! To the villages, the hovels, the farthest squat huts. Promise them riches, royal favors, whatever it takes! There must be someone in the kingdom who can bring this plant back to life!

ROCCO

You heard him, move out.

(Rocco sends the gardeners out and a new batch files in, which can be the exact same performers with more rustic hats. At the tail end of their procession is a hunched old gardener, her face obscured by her cloak. These new gardeners puzzle and fuss as more days pass.)

TRUFFALDINO

Lured by the promise of riches, the best gardeners in the kingdom came to try their luck but nothing worked. One by one they gave up the task as hopeless.

(Gardeners give up and abandon the project one by one until the hunched gardener is the only one left.)

LORENZO

Wait! Where are you all going? The myrtle! You must save it!

ROCCO

It's not happening. Can't you just get a new one?

LORENZO

I could search the world over and never find a tree the equal of this one. We'll keep searching. There must be someone who--

ROCCO

They all gave up. Except for that one old thing that's been sitting there so long I'm not even sure it's still alive.

LORENZO

Yehk.

(He closes the balcony curtain on it.)

ROCCO

You want my professional opinion?

LORENZO

What is it?

ROCCO

It's dead, yo.

LORENZO

My position if not my very life depends on reviving this myrtle!

ROCCO

Sucks to be you.

LORENZO

You are supremely unhelpful.

(With a shrug, Rocco leaves, passing Prince Cola on his way in.)

SCENE 11

PRINCE COLA

Rocco? What are you-- Lorenzo!

LORENZO

Prince Cola? You're, uh, home so soon!

PRINCE COLA

I found the cottage in Miano but it was abandoned, the garden wild and overgrown. I was suddenly overcome with a terrible foreboding. I had to return straight away.

LORENZO

Well, after so long a journey surely you'll want a wash, some fresh clothes--

PRINCE COLA

I want for nothing but to see my beloved myrtle again.

(He starts for the balcony, but Lorenzo blocks his path.)

LORENZO

No, please, your majesty. I beg of you, give me a little more time so that I may--

PRINCE COLA

What is the meaning of this? Let me pass!

(Lorenzo drops to his knees, begging at the prince's hem.)

LORENZO

Prince Cola, please, I throw myself upon your mercy. I know not what happened and I have done everything in my power to try to repair it without success, but your myrtle is--

(The myrtle fairy emerges from the balcony.)

PRINCE COLA

There!

LORENZO

What?

PRINCE COLA

My love, I had such a terrible feeling of dread as I rode back but yet here you are.

MYRTLE

I was so cold. Those women they... Oh, my love! I had the most terrible nightmare.

(She falls into his arms.)

LORENZO

I have clearly missed something.

PRINCE COLA

The myrtle, Lorenzo. She's to be my bride!

LORENZO

You're marrying a tree?

MYRTLE

I am only the tree in sunlight.

LORENZO

You're the... But it... Ah. They must have throttled me so hard when they found out about the myrtle that now I'm hallucinating. Yes, yes, let's just shut the whole thing down. Much better that way...

(He faints.)

PRINCE COLA

Oh, my love, how I have missed you. Now that I am with you I curse every blink that does interrupt the viewing of your beauty. What sky is missing the celestial orbs that became your bright eyes? What sea waves sadly at the beach that held the shells that became your delicate ears? What master craftsman did shape your body like a--

MYRTLE

OK, you need to stop.

PRINCE COLA

Right. Sorry.

MYRTLE

I have read your stories. I know humans can be bewitched by our looks. But I need to be certain you care for me and not just the crown of soft curls. I believe you understand this well, Prince Cola.

PRINCE COLA

So you do know. I never meant to deceive you. It's only--

LORENZO
(wakes suddenly)
Wait a minute! The myrtle tree was dead! I had every gardener in the land in here, and they swore it was a hopeless case.

MYRTLE

You mean to say... it was not a nightmare? But then how--

(The hunched gardener comes in from the balcony.)

LORENZO

You! This is the one who saved the day, your highness. You should make her the new royal gardener because that other guy is the worst.

PRINCE COLA

If this is true, anything in my kingdom is yours, stranger, for restoring my myrtle to me.

(The hunched gardener reveals herself to be La Giardiniera.)

LA GIARDINIERA

I restored her to herself, young man.

MYRTLE

Mama!

LA GIARDINIERA

I have found you, little one. At last.

(They hug.)
So, you're in love with the prince, are you? Even without a monster for a father-in-law, you'll never have a moment's peace, not between balls

and duties and jealous suitors. Are you sure you want to bind yourself to all that?

MYRTLE

Mama--

PRINCE COLA

No, she's right. About my father, the duties, the suitors, all of it. I am the man you knew in these rooms, but I'm also a prince with everything that comes with that. I'm cursed too, in a way.

MYRTLE

I am not cursed. This is no enchantment to break. The plant and I are one, and that will always be so. This is my life.

LA GIARDINIERA

And it ain't easy!

MYRTLE

No, it isn't. This is as normal as it can ever be between us.

PRINCE COLA

I don't care. That is what I wanted to say earlier. I am not bewitched. I love you as you are, fairy and flowers, inside and out.

(She takes his hands)

MYRTLE

The good and the bad.

LA GIARDINIERA

That's how it should be. A plant needs both sunshine and rain to grow. It's just the same with love.

(King comes in his robe)

KING

What is all this blasted yakking when I'm trying to sleep? I'll have you all hung.

PRINCE COLA

Father! I'd like to introduce you to my fiancée.

(King thinks he's talking about La Giardiniera.)

KING

This old bird?

LA GIARDINIERA

Better an old bird than a gold boar.

KING

Ha! I like her!

PRINCE COLA

No, father, this is my fiancée.

MYRTLE

Your highness.

(She curtsies.)

KING

Oh. She's alright too I guess. Doesn't matter much to me so long as she starts popping out heirs in good time.

PRINCE COLA

Gah! Why are you like this?

KING

It's what I'm like, boy! Deal with it. That's the point you were all moseying around to in here anyway, isn't it?

LA GIARDINIERA

A seed grows what it grows. All you can do is your best to tend the plant you've got.

KING

See? Well, go on. You got us all up out of bed, now you two might as well make it all official.

(The prince and myrtle kiss.)

There! Now I gotta get the taste of all this sentimentality out of my mouth. I'm going down to the kitchen to yell until someone gets me some ham. Who's coming?

(Exit.)

TRUFFALDINO

The lovers were married at once. When the new princess spotted Vendramina and the other treacherous sisters at the wedding feast, the prince tricked them into naming their own punishment and had them buried al--

(He glances at the audience.)

...a lot later in life... after some years in prison. Or something. Anyway, they all, well most of them anyway, lived happily ever after.

(He shuts the book)

There, see? That wasn't so bad. Makes you wonder what other halfway decent stories you've been ignoring for the usual suspects, doesn't it? Well, that's it for me. It's time to go downstairs, kick up my feet and bust out the good snacks. You little monsters go to sleep. Nighty night!

(Exit.)

ALSO BY HILLARY DEPIANO

HILLARYDEPIANO.COM

FULL LENGTH PLAYS

THE LOVE OF THREE ORANGES
comedy / fantasy /commedia dell'arte
90 to 120 minutes, 8 f, 8 m, 5 any (13-40+ actors possible: 7-20 f, 5-20 m)
A prince is cursed to fall in love with three magical oranges.

THE GREEN BIRD
comedy / fantasy /commedia dell'arte
90 to 120 minutes, 4 m 6 f 3 any (13-40+ actors possible)
Four royals, two clowns, and way too many talking statues must unravel the
mystery of the green bird before an evil queen destroys the kingdom.

ONE ACT PLAYS

DADDY ISSUES
drama
15 to 20 minutes, 1 female, 1 male, 3 any
A young woman must confront the ghost of her past.

POLAR TWILIGHT
comedy / holiday
20 to 25 minutes, 3 f, 3 m (6 actors possible: 0-5 f, 1-6 m)
Everything you know about Santa is wrong and the truth kind of... sucks.
Vampire Santa Claus... but in a cute way!

NEW YEAR'S THIEVE
comedy / holiday
30 to 35 minutes, 2 m 3 f 3 any (7 to 10+ actors possible)
Someone's stolen the New Year and the main suspect is... Frosty the coat
rack?

WEAK DAYS
comedy
45 to 60 minutes, 6-7 any
All five weekdays play out at simultaneously across the stage in a comic
ballet. Winner of The Chameleon Theatre Circle's 16th Annual New Play
Contest.

THE LOVE OF THREE ORANGES (ONE ACT VERSION)
comedy / fantasy /commedia dell'arte
35 to 40 minutes, 8 f, 6 m, 4 any (10-30+ actors possible)
A prince is cursed to fall in love with three magical oranges.

THE GREEN BIRD (ONE ACT VERSION)

comedy / fantasy /commedia dell'arte
35 to 45 minutes, 4 m 6 f 3 any (12-40+ actors possible)
Four royals, two clowns, and way too many talking statues must unravel the mystery of the green bird before an evil queen destroys the kingdom.

SHORT PLAYS (10-15 MINUTES)
THE RAVEN / LENORE
THE THREE LITTLE PIGS AND THE BIG BAD STORM
THE (COMPLETELY INACCURATE) LEGEND OF THE MUMMY WITCH
HOUSE
MASKS
THE COMPLETE NOVELS OF JANE AUSTEN: NOW NEW AND IMPROVED!
THREE PADDED WALLS

OTHER FICTION AND NON-FICTION
NANO WHAT NOW?
Finding your editing process, revising your NaNoWriMo book and building a writing career through publishing and beyond.
THE AUTHOR
(award winning novella) You ever get the feeling you don't know which side of the pen you're on?

~

WRITING AS T. W. SELLER
THEWHINESELLER.COM
SELL THEIR STUFF
From eBay Trading Assistants to multichannel seller assistance, your ultimate guide to consignment selling online as a part-time income or full-time business
EBAY MARKETING MAKEOVER
Increase sales and grow traffic to your eBay items by encouraging word of mouth, focusing on your ideal buyers, and optimizing your selling for search and mobile
BEYOND AMAZON, EBAY, AND ETSY
Free and low cost alternative marketplaces, shopping cart solutions and e-commerce storefronts
THE SELLER LEDGER
An auction organizer for selling on eBay

ABOUT THE AUTHOR

Hillary DePiano is a playwright, fiction and non-fiction author best known for fantastically funny fairy tales, surprisingly sweet slapstick and unrelentingly upbeat writing advice. With over two dozen plays for everyone from pre-schoolers and up, she's honored to have had her work performed in schools and theatres around the world.

As the author of the *How to Start Writing* series, she regularly shares advice and pep as a blogger and speaker. Since 2010, Hillary heads the Northeastern New Jersey region for NaNoWriMo.org and works as a volunteer in support of their creative mission. She also writes about eBay, e-commerce, and selling online under the name T. W. Seller at TheWhineSeller.com.

For more information about her books, plays, and blogs or to connect via social media, visit HillaryDePiano.com.